Acting Edition

MW01068682

Witch

by Jen Silverman

‖ SAMUEL FRENCH ‖

Copyright © 2022 by Jen Silverman
All Rights Reserved

WITCH is fully protected under the copyright laws of the United States of America, the British Commonwealth, including Canada, and all member countries of the Berne Convention for the Protection of Literary and Artistic Works, the Universal Copyright Convention, and/or the World Trade Organization conforming to the Agreement on Trade Related Aspects of Intellectual Property Rights. All rights, including professional and amateur stage productions, recitation, lecturing, public reading, motion picture, radio broadcasting, television, online/digital production, and the rights of translation into foreign languages are strictly reserved.

ISBN 978-0-573-70823-7

www.concordtheatricals.com
www.concordtheatricals.co.uk

FOR PRODUCTION INQUIRIES

UNITED STATES AND CANADA
info@concordtheatricals.com
1-866-979-0447

UNITED KINGDOM AND EUROPE
licensing@concordtheatricals.co.uk
020-7054-7298

Each title is subject to availability from Concord Theatricals Corp., depending upon country of performance. Please be aware that *WITCH* may not be licensed by Concord Theatricals Corp. in your territory. Professional and amateur producers should contact the nearest Concord Theatricals Corp. office or licensing partner to verify availability.

CAUTION: Professional and amateur producers are hereby warned that *WITCH* is subject to a licensing fee. The purchase, renting, lending or use of this book does not constitute a license to perform this title(s), which license must be obtained from Concord Theatricals Corp. prior to any performance. Performance of this title(s) without a license is a violation of federal law and may subject the producer and/or presenter of such performances to civil penalties. Both amateurs and professionals considering a production are strongly advised to apply to the appropriate agent before starting rehearsals, advertising, or booking a theatre. A licensing fee must be paid whether the title(s) is presented for charity or gain and whether or not admission is charged. Professional/Stock licensing fees are quoted upon application to Concord Theatricals Corp.

This work is published by Samuel French, an imprint of Concord Theatricals Corp.

No one shall make any changes in this title(s) for the purpose of production. No part of this book may be reproduced, stored in a retrieval system, scanned, uploaded, or transmitted in any form, by any means, now known or yet to be invented, including mechanical, electronic, digital, photocopying, recording, videotaping, or otherwise, without the prior written permission of the publisher. No one shall share this title(s), or any part of this title(s), through any social media or file hosting websites.

For all inquiries regarding motion picture, television, online/digital and other media rights, please contact Concord Theatricals Corp.

MUSIC AND THIRD-PARTY MATERIALS USE NOTE

Licensees are solely responsible for obtaining formal written permission from copyright owners to use copyrighted music and/or other copyrighted third-party materials (e.g., artworks, logos) in the performance of this play and are strongly cautioned to do so. If no such permission is obtained by the licensee, then the licensee must use only original music and materials that the licensee owns and controls. Licensees are solely responsible and liable for clearances of all third-party copyrighted materials, including without limitation music, and shall indemnify the copyright owners of the play(s) and their licensing agent, Concord Theatricals Corp., against any costs, expenses, losses and liabilities arising from the use of such copyrighted third-party materials by licensees. For music, please contact the appropriate music licensing authority in your territory for the rights to any incidental music.

IMPORTANT BILLING AND CREDIT REQUIREMENTS

If you have obtained performance rights to this title, please refer to your licensing agreement for important billing and credit requirements.

WITCH was commissioned by Writers Theatre through the Literary Development Initiative, with the generous support of David and Mary Winton Green, and the world premiere was presented at Writers Theatre in Glencoe, Illinois (Michael Halberstam, Artistic Director; Kathryn M. Lipuma, Executive Director) on September 27, 2018. The production was directed by Marti Lyons, with choreography by Katie Spelman, scenic design by Yu Shibagaki, costume design by Mieka van der Ploeg, sound design by Mikhail Fiksel, and lighting design by Paul Toben. The stage manager was Cara Parrish. The cast was as follows:

ELIZABETH SAWYER. . . . . Audrey Francis

SCRATCH . . . . Ryan Hallahan

SIR ARTHUR BANKS. . . . . David Alan Anderson

CUDDY BANKS . . . . Steve Haggard

FRANK THORNEY. . . . . Jon Hudson Odom

WINNIFRED . . . . Arti Ishak

CHARACTERS

ELIZABETH SAWYER – (female, forties/fifties/sixties) An outcast.

SCRATCH – (male, twenties/early thirties) The devil.

SIR ARTHUR BANKS – (male, fifties/sixties) A wealthy and powerful man.

CUDDY BANKS – (male, twenties/early thirties) Sir Arthur's son, painfully shy, a Morris dancer. He is secretly in love with Frank (and also in hate).

FRANK THORNEY – (male, twenties/early thirties) A confident and successful young man, charming and ruthless. His ambition knows no bounds.

WINNIFRED – (female, twenties/early thirties) Sir Arthur's servant, resigned and pragmatic, secretly married to Frank.

SETTING

The Village of Edmonton: a semi-rural small town lost in the country.

TIME

Then-ish. But equally of our moment. No faux-period accents, please.

AUTHOR'S NOTES

The spacing is a gesture toward indicating rhythm and how thoughts change, morph, contradict each other, escalate, or get supplanted by other thoughts as we talk. The line breaks often signal either an intensification of, or a shift away, from something. It <u>does not</u> indicate a beat or pause except where written.

[ ]	is unspoken, although the character is thinking it.
( )	is spoken out loud, but is a side-thought.
/	signifies an interruption, where the / occurs.

Each of the characters has what is referred to as an "**aria**." This is not about increased "lyricism" or a heightened style. In these arias, an urgency takes hold, a spilling out of deeply buried things – a churning engine of truth.

Casting

These characters can be played by actors of any ethnicity. Sir Arthur and his son Cuddy do not have to be played by actors of the same ethnicity.

1.

(**ELIZABETH SAWYER**. *Alone. A light tight on her face. Her aria. A moment out of time.*)

ELIZABETH. I'm not arguing for the end of the world but then again maybe I am.
This one, anyway.

I imagine you're not sure about this,
you might think I'm jumping the gun.
Fair enough, full disclosure –
wherever I go, people are like:
"Oh there's the witch of Edmonton."
They're like: "You made my cow sick, you made my thatch burn."
I'm like a disease that only I seem to have caught.
I'm like a plague of locusts that's just one locust.
And the whispering!
Say I'm in line at the well.
If I turn around, the whispering stops. Dead silence.
But somehow it always starts up again.

I can't say I don't have a grudge, because
I do, clearly, I do have a grudge.
But does that detract from my argument, or is it just added texture?

I understand – you're hesitating right now,
you're like: *Is she kidding, is she serious, is she crazy,*
– and those are questions, they are valid questions,
but they are not the *right* questions.
Here is the single thing you should be asking yourself:

Do I have hope that things can get better?

And if you do, then ignore me. You're fine.
But if you don't…
then maybe this is where we start.

2.

(A bar. **SCRATCH** *and* **CUDDY BANKS.***)*

(Back in the flow of time.)

CUDDY. The devil?

SCRATCH. Your soul, blood-pact, endless riches.

CUDDY. Endless?

SCRATCH. Power: reckless, abusable. Fame!

CUDDY. Fame?

SCRATCH. Have to pick, can't have it all, but sure, fame.

CUDDY. Huh.

> *(Pause.)*

I don't know why you're coming to me. I've never even gotten in trouble with the law.

SCRATCH. But you want to.

CUDDY. But I haven't.

SCRATCH. *(Shrugs, easy.)* I'm just as interested in what you *want* as what you *do*.

CUDDY. You been to my father's place?

SCRATCH. Nah.

CUDDY. Sir Arthur, he owns the castle.

SCRATCH. Nope.

CUDDY. He's super important, everybody knows him.

SCRATCH. No.

CUDDY. My dad is a real son-of-a-bitch, you haven't been to his place?

SCRATCH. He lacks imagination.

CUDDY. *(A little flattered.)* ...Oh.

SCRATCH. *You*, on the other hand, have potential.

   *(***CUDDY*** gets a little excited by this.)*

CUDDY. I perform in a Morris troupe, actually, if you want to know. Me and my friends do Morris dancing, maybe you've heard of us, maybe you've seen us, maybe –

SCRATCH. I didn't mean the dancing.

CUDDY. ...Oh.

SCRATCH. Although it's good to have hobbies.

CUDDY. It's not a hobby, I keep – [having to explain that]
My dad says that all the time too, I'm like
Dad
this is not a *hobby*
this is *my life*.

SCRATCH. – Of course.

CUDDY. The Morris dance is very intricate
very raw and intricate.
It's like...seriously underrated.

SCRATCH. I stand corrected.

   (Pause.)

CUDDY. Who else have you been to?

SCRATCH. In my lifetime? In the world?

CUDDY. In Edmonton.
(This is loaded.) Frank Thorney?

SCRATCH. Who?

CUDDY. *(In love and equally in hate.)* Everybody is all, "Ooh Frank Thorney."
My dad is like, obsessed with Frank Thorney.

He found him working in a field and like, took him to
our castle
and for the past five years he's always like,
"You should go hiking, Frank loves the outdoors,"
"You should eat more meat, Frank eats meat,"
"You should go on more dates, girls love Frank,"
and it's like, uhh, hello, I'm your *son*
what's the BFD with Frank??

>   *(Beat.)*

So...in the whole town, just me?

SCRATCH. You're one of the few.

CUDDY. *(He's never been special before.)* Oh...

>   *(Then – jealous.)* Who are the others?

SCRATCH. Does it matter?

CUDDY. The old witch Sawyer?
I bet it's Sawyer.

SCRATCH. Why do you say that?

CUDDY. Everyone says she makes the crops wither.
Everyone says she makes the cows dry up.
Everyone says she dances with the devil in the pale
moonlight.
And that's you, right? So...

>   *(**SCRATCH** sees **CUDDY**'s insecurity and
>   prepares for the kill.)*

SCRATCH. I can't confirm or deny that right now, Cuddy.

CUDDY. Do you guys hang out all the time?
Do you, like, fly around on her broomstick together?
Just nod your head.
If it's Yes just look to the right.
Or if it's Yes, cough twice.
Or if it's Yes –

SCRATCH. The real question at hand is: what do *you* want?

CUDDY. …Me?

SCRATCH. Some men want wealth. Some men want land. And some men…many men…want love.

> (**CUDDY** *hastens to dispatch this train of thought.*)

CUDDY. There's this girl, Winnifred, we're basically a thing. She works in my castle and
she's like…*drawn* to me
like an animal thing
so.

> (*A beat. As sympathetically as possible:*)

SCRATCH. Huh.

CUDDY. What.

SCRATCH. Hmm.

CUDDY. What??

SCRATCH. Well
I hate to say this but
there's a slight problem with Winnifred.

CUDDY. There is?

SCRATCH. Winnifred is secretly married to Young Frank Thorney. So. Winnifred might be *drawn* to you. That's certainly possible. But she can't be your girlfriend…or your wife…which is a problem, considering the rumors. But maybe you don't care about the rumors.

CUDDY. (*A little pale.*) What rumors.

SCRATCH. They're stupid. Don't worry about them. Your father is just a little concerned, that's all about his heir

getting married and *producing* an heir
he's just a little anxious that your favorite flavor might
not be "wife"
if you get what I'm saying.

> *(A beat.)*

CUDDY. That's ridiculous.

SCRATCH. I'm sure it is! I'm sure it's ridiculous.
It's just
adoption is a word that
one hears floated, from time to time,
in these circumstances.

CUDDY. Adoption?

SCRATCH. Frank as the
"Adoptive Heir"...you know
but:
Rumor! Rumor.
Probably untrue.

CUDDY. Frank Thorney??
I *hate* Frank Thorney!

> *(This gets more intense as it goes.)*

My dad gave him a horse and now he goes everywhere
by horseback! It's like, you have legs, can't you walk?
It's like, you're going three feet, just fucking walk! But
nope, there's Frank Thorney on his goddamn horse.
And I'm like, Hi Frank, and he always just *looks* at me,
he just *looks* at me, and then he keeps going. And I'm
like, Bye Frank. I'm like, your dad is a farmer, Frank!
I'm like, fuck you Frank! I'm like, someday I'm gonna
punch you in your perfectly-straight teeth, someday
I'm gonna be like Hi Frank and then I'm gonna hit
you so hard you fall off that stupid fucking horse and
I'm gonna keep hitting you and keep hitting you and

keep hitting you until all those straight square teeth are bashed into your stupid beautiful face and I'm gonna say BYE FRANK BYE FRANK BYEEEEE FRAAAAANK!

> *(A beat.* **CUDDY** *is breathing really hard. He gets it together. He is ashamed, and also liberated. He looks at* **SCRATCH.** **SCRATCH***'s face is encouraging. A long beat.)*

You can have my soul.

I want you to kill Frank.

SCRATCH. I think we can make that work.

3.

*(**SCRATCH** and **FRANK**. Possibly the same bar.)*

FRANK. *Who* did you say you were?

SCRATCH. *(A bow.)* Your servant.

FRANK. Have we met?

SCRATCH. I think we have some friends in common, Frank
    Thorney.

FRANK. Is that so?

SCRATCH. Up in the castle, for example,
    I think a number of our friends in the castle
    are friends in common.

*(**FRANK**'s demeanor changes completely.)*

FRANK. Oh! well
    you do look a little familiar to me
    we must have run into each other at a banquet,
    perhaps?
    Maybe at a banquet.

SCRATCH. Yes, maybe at a banquet.

FRANK. How long are you in town for?

SCRATCH. Oh, just sort of – making the rounds.
    Everybody's very impressed with you, you know.

FRANK. *(This means a lot.)* Is that so?

SCRATCH. Your bearing, your stature, your grace. Everybody's
    impressed.

FRANK. Oh that's very kind, that's very kind.
    (Who said that?)

SCRATCH. Sir Arthur,
    Sir Arthur thinks a lot of you
    as I'm sure you're aware.

FRANK. Oh! well he's become just like a father to me.

SCRATCH. And Young Cuddy.

FRANK. Who?

SCRATCH. Young Cuddy of the Morris dancers.

FRANK. Who?

SCRATCH. Sir Arthur's only son?

FRANK. Oh...*him.*

SCRATCH. Also Winnifred.

FRANK. *(Uneasy.)* ...Who?

SCRATCH. And I can't tell you how many parents have said to me, "Frank Thorney has turned out so well, Frank Thorney is the model for how we raise our children."

FRANK. Do people say that?

SCRATCH. Of course, there are things they don't know. But isn't that always the case?

FRANK. ...I'm sorry?

SCRATCH. What is a town without its secrets? Its secret hates, its secret loves...its secret marriages.

FRANK. ...Who did you say you were?

SCRATCH. Oh! Sorry, my apologies.
Can't believe it slipped my mind.
I'm the devil.

(A beat. **FRANK** *gets very eager and excited.)*

FRANK. Oh! I know this part!

SCRATCH. You do?

FRANK. This is the part where you tempt me! And I say No,
because I'm good, because I'm the hero,
always been a special child, poor but virtuous,
sort of a Noble Working Class Individual,

and my mother always said to me:

"Frank, you must be the example for your brothers and sisters,"

and I *was*

(and I was also very good at sports) –

(that was later on)

– (and horseback riding),

(also later on) –

and so my whole life, really, people have been holding me up and saying:

Look at Frank.

Sort of saying: *He's special.*

And I know that they're right,

there's something inside me that's incredibly rare and incredibly special,

and it is my job to *foster* that thing,

encourage that thing,

and even when we had nothing to eat, my mother always said:

"Frank, you are destined for greatness,"

and so here you are, and it's your job to say: "Frank, let me tear you down."

But it's *my* job to say No, and so the answer is...

NO.

    (A real beat.)

You're still here.

SCRATCH. I'm just hanging out.

FRANK. I said No, so why are you still here?

SCRATCH. Well, I didn't offer you anything.

FRANK. ...I'm sorry?

SCRATCH. I'm not offering you anything. I hear your No and I respect your No and I'm not trying to devalue the power of your No, but I actually didn't make you an offer.

FRANK. Oh.

SCRATCH. Don't feel bad or anything.

FRANK. *(Starting to feel bad.)* I'm not.

SCRATCH. Don't feel left out at all, it's nothing personal.

FRANK. *(Feeling left out.)* No no, I'm not.

SCRATCH. And you shouldn't, because you would have said No anyway, if I'd offered you anything you wouldn't have taken it. You have way more going for you than Cuddy Banks.

FRANK. *(A little horrified.)* Cuddy Banks?

SCRATCH. You remember…

FRANK. You made *him* some sort of…offer?

SCRATCH. I mean, it's funny because he has wealth, he has the title, he'll inherit his father's land – so it's funny to think about, because Cuddy actually has all the things a man could want, but I guess once you have everything, you just want more. Whereas *you* don't really have anything, but you're fine.

FRANK. What do you mean I don't have *anything*?

SCRATCH. Oh! I'm so sorry, maybe I misunderstood the situation?
The way it sounded – from you and others, mostly from others – it sounded like you come from a poor family and they don't have anything to give you – except debt, probably, probably there's a lot of debt – and you live in the castle due to Sir Arthur's goodwill right *now*, but, you know, eventually he'll die, and everything will go to Cuddy, so…that will be really shitty, when the time comes. But I feel like you're being really zen about the whole thing, which is so impressive.

> *(Something in **FRANK** changes. A glimmer of the ruthless hunger that is always just underneath his polished surface.)*

FRANK. All right.

SCRATCH. All right?

FRANK. I want to be heir.
The castle, the title, the land.
You can have my soul.

(**SCRATCH** *smiles. He takes a sip of his drink.*)

SCRATCH. I think we can make that work.

4.

(**ELIZABETH**'s *country cottage. Shabby, poor.*)

(**SCRATCH** *has just arrived.*)

ELIZABETH. The devil?

SCRATCH. Blah blah blah your soul etc.

ELIZABETH. *My* soul?

SCRATCH. Ripe for the picking.

ELIZABETH. Why *mine*?

SCRATCH. Everybody says you're a witch.
You're not, of course. But! would you like to be?

ELIZABETH. I was warned about you.

SCRATCH. Everybody is warned about me, it doesn't seem
to make much of a difference.
Mind if I sit down?

ELIZABETH. As a matter of fact, Yes.

SCRATCH. *(Coaxing.)* Offer me a drink. Common courtesy!
Can't hurt, can it?

ELIZABETH. Nobody sits in my cabin but me.

(*A moment.* **SCRATCH** *elaborately leans but
doesn't sit.*)

SCRATCH. How would you like me to fuck up some people
for you.
How would you like...revenge.

ELIZABETH. You want me to sell you my soul.
Men make it sound like they're doing you a favor when
what they really want is a favor done for them.

SCRATCH. Astute! That's very astute, and I hear you. But I would say – think of it as more an exchange between friends.

Think of it kind of like a pot-luck.

ELIZABETH. *(Despite herself.)* ...A "pot-luck"?

SCRATCH. A pot-luck is what happens in the future, when people don't worry about food.

And instead of everybody just eating their own food as fast as they can find it, people get together, usually outside, usually somewhere uncomfortable and on a patio and with too many bugs, and everybody pretends not to notice how many bugs there are, they talk about the sunset, and they eat each other's food. Slowly. Over a great deal of time. And everybody wants to go home long before they actually do.

ELIZABETH. Oh.

SCRATCH. Something to look forward to!

You could practice, with me.

I bring power and reckless lack of consequence. You bring your soul.

(A beat.)

ELIZABETH. If I "pot-luck" my soul...

SCRATCH. Yes?

ELIZABETH. – And that's a big *if* –

SCRATCH. – Pure hypotheticals, I understand –

ELIZABETH. What do I get?

SCRATCH. Oh! Well that's an easy one. That's where it gets easy.

ELIZABETH. Okay...

SCRATCH. You tell me. The villagers who are cruel to you? Make a list. Their cows get pox. The girls who giggle behind their hands? Warts on the hands. I mean, it all sort of depends on you, at that point.

ELIZABETH. And what would you do with it? My soul?

SCRATCH. What have *you* done with it so far?

ELIZABETH. Nothing much, I guess.

SCRATCH. Then you won't miss it.

ELIZABETH. Nobody wakes up in the middle of the night? Nobody gets an earache or a toothache or a weird uncanny ache-ache that won't seem to go away?

SCRATCH. Nobody's reported those kinds of symptoms.

ELIZABETH. Oh.

SCRATCH. So, what do you think?

ELIZABETH. Can I change my mind? If I say Yes, can I change it back?

SCRATCH. Oh! no. No no. No take-backs.

ELIZABETH. And what if I say No?

SCRATCH. You know, people ask me this sometimes. And my sort of standard – the answer I like to give – I mean, I can get dramatic, I can be like: *I tear you apart, I rip you limb from* – you know? – *I burn your entire* – like, I can do that, but honestly, the answer I like to give is: I leave. I just leave. And your entire life continues on, exactly as it was, zero change, as if I were never here. And one day, maybe next week or maybe ten years from now...or maybe on your death-bed... One day you ask yourself why is it that you have been so relentlessly miserable, why is it that you never ever, not even once, had the chance to make yourself less unhappy. And then at that moment, whenever it comes, you think of this. You think of this conversation. And you think: *Oh. I did have the chance. I did have it. I just said No.*

(A long beat. And then:)

ELIZABETH. No thank you.

5.

(Sir Arthur's banquet hall, in the aftermath of a great banquet. A portrait of his dead wife hangs above the proceedings.)

*(***SIR ARTHUR** *is in his great banquet chair, holding court.* **CUDDY** *and* **FRANK** *are to his sides. There's huge tension in the air. Each one is on the edge, waiting for the moment in which his world will change.)*

*(***WINNIFRED** *cleans up the banquet. She walks past them, weighed down with heavy dishes – sumptuous, obscene platters, tureens, etc.* **WINNIFRED** *walks all the way from one side of the stage to the other. Then a long pause while she off-loads dishes and gets more. Then she walks past us again.)*

(Every so often, **SIR ARTHUR** *will call to* **WINNIFRED***, and then she will break her pattern and hurry over with the thing he requests. Then back to her pattern.)*

SIR ARTHUR. And the thing is: the free market. You know?

FRANK. (Certainly, certainly.)

SIR ARTHUR. And one wants to *celebrate* the free market, one wants to
embrace the possibility of a world in which anyone, any man,
(no matter his background)
can *succeed.*

FRANK. (Absolutely.)

SIR ARTHUR. So that's just, that's just one way of –
But then there's the issue of *legacy.* / You know?

FRANK. Yes, legacy is crucial –

SIR ARTHUR. Then there's the issue of – what you hand
down.
What you are directly responsible for.
(Winnifred!)
(Winnifred, hand-wipes!)

> *(Back to the* **BOYS.***)*

For example, if you raise your children right, they have
a sense of
I don't know, *responsibility* toward the world.
You have *handed down* your sense of –
(Thank you, Winnifred.)

> *(***WINNIFRED** *has brought hand-wipes. She
> stands by patiently while the* **MEN** *take turns
> using them. She's mostly ignored.)*

FRANK. Absolutely sir, I think it's all about values.

SIR ARTHUR. Values, yes, values.

FRANK. And inheritance confirms values. You know?
Who you leave it all to is about what you *value*.

CUDDY. (Ohhhkay...)

FRANK. For example, a person who works hard, who gets
ahead,
that's a person who you could sort of trust, trust with
a legacy,
because *his* values and *your* values –

SIR ARTHUR. Everybody thinks it's about class, but it's
about *values*.

FRANK. I couldn't agree more, sir, truly.

SIR ARTHUR. Your father raised *you* with the right values
and you weren't   [rich]
ya know, you didn't have   [things easy]

but look at you!
You're a bright young man, you're moving in the
right   [direction]
not *victimized* by your previous hardships
and maybe those hardships *are* a legacy –

> *(Now we're getting somewhere! And they're
> riffing together.)*

FRANK. – Of experience, of authentic experience –

SIR ARTHUR. – The means by which one gains a sense of
self –

FRANK. – Hardship as a valued teacher, really –

SIR ARTHUR. *(Likes this a lot.)* – Hardship *equals* value –

FRANK. – Value *equals* legacy, *equals* inheritance –

> *(**FRANK** pops a grape in his mouth...and
> chokes on it. **CUDDY** sits up expectantly,
> waiting for **FRANK** to keel over. **FRANK** coughs
> mightily...but does not.)*

CUDDY. *(Here we go!)* He's choking!

SIR ARTHUR. He's fine.

FRANK. I'm fine.

CUDDY. *(Subsides, disappointed.)* Oh.

FRANK. Just got a little over-excited.

SIR ARTHUR. Very exciting stuff, values, legacy, very exciting.

> *(Well, if **FRANK** isn't currently dying, and
> we are still all having this conversation...
> **CUDDY** feels the need to assert himself.)*

CUDDY. OK, I just,
I *also* wouldn't say that someone who lives in a castle
doesn't have hardship.

SIR ARTHUR. Oh?

FRANK. *Oh*-kay.

CUDDY. What.

FRANK. I mean
the "poor little rich kid" argument
we've all...   [heard that before]

CUDDY. "Poor little" –? What's that *even* –

FRANK. The whole thing about emotional hollowness,
emotional lack
but I mean, once you put that up against *actual* lack –
Lack of resources, lack of food, lack of shelter –
Emotional lack seems...well, lacking.

> (**SIR ARTHUR** *breaks in, as things are getting savage.*)

SIR ARTHUR. Love a lively conversation! Gets the digestion
going!

CUDDY. Well Frank.
It's interesting to *me* that you seem to have such a
connection to the idea of *actual* lack
when you've spent the past five years living here at the
castle
and wearing my dad's clothes and eating my dad's food
and
you know, riding a horse my dad *gave* you and like
I guess I just don't see what you're lacking...*physically.*

FRANK. Excuse me?

SIR ARTHUR. We've been fortunate, have a good kid – good
man – around –

CUDDY. Sure, I mean sure, but I'm just interested in
Frank's opinions on hardship
because I understand that his background was perhaps,
ah, underprivileged
but he has certainly been blessed with *access*, hasn't he.

FRANK. *(Tight and a little raw.)* Well, Cuddy
I would never fail to acknowledge that your dad
changed my life –

SIR ARTHUR. *(Modest, a little embarrassed, but pleased.)*
(Oh now...)

FRANK. *(This comes from a place of truth.)* – But I
think maybe *your* privilege makes it hard for you to
understand that five years of this doesn't quite override
twenty years of having nothing. *You* might forget to eat
lunch, say you're at Morris-dancing practice and you
forget lunch, and then you come into the kitchen, you
say, "I'm starving!" – you have no idea what starving is
like. You have no idea. If you did, you wouldn't think
that twenty years of starvation could be forgotten after
one big meal.

> *(SIR ARTHUR is moved and surprised. He interjects:)*

SIR ARTHUR. Well-spoken, Frank.

(Afterthought.) – *And* Cuddy! and Cuddy –

(Smoothing it all over.) Think it's good for men to
practice the art of dissent.

FRANK. Thank you.

CUDDY. Thanks.

SIR ARTHUR. Argument used to be an art you know
Ancient Greeks and
Syrians? probably the Syrians?
Mesopotamia!
(where's Mesopotamia?)
Here, have a date
have a fresh date
Winnifred!

> *(WINNIFRED comes running.)*

A date!

(WINNIFRED holds out a bowl of dates. Dismissing her:)

(thank you Winnifred)
anyway
advanced civilizations train their young men to argue
to think like lawyers, but with *heart*
lawyer-poets
think we miss that, nowadays
violence and
think we miss that.

(With increasing nostalgia that kind of takes him over:)

Cuddy's mom was a real...
she could argue like a man
she could look you straight in the eyes and just
decimate your argument
just tear you apart in a thousand ways and –

(This has gone to an unexpectedly lonely place.)

I loved being decimated by her.

(And then SIR ARTHUR rallies. Back to normal! Addressing FRANK:)

I don't say this lightly, young man, but
I have some friends whose daughters
are a little higher in station than you might normally –
but I think with my strong advocacy, you might be able
to –
you know, just sort of, get some irons in the fire.

(WINNIFRED is shooting FRANK glares over the dishes.)

FRANK. *(This is a Yes.)* I couldn't possibly impose on you, sir.

SIR ARTHUR. Not an imposition at all! Not at all!
(Winnifred! A digestif!)

> (**WINNIFRED** *comes over with a bottle.*)

Wish young Cuddy would let his old dad *impose*
but happy to, happy to.
You know, actually Frank, I've been thinking –

FRANK. ...Yes??

> (**WINNIFRED** *pours the digestif in* **FRANK***'s lap.*)

Hey!!

SIR ARTHUR. Watch what you're doing, girl!

WINNIFRED. Sorry. I'm so sorry.
I slipped.

> (*She dabs at* **FRANK***'s lap. He can't look at her.*)

FRANK. It's fine, it's fine.

WINNIFRED. Sorry.

FRANK. It's OK, that's enough.

CUDDY. It's not like he *drowned*.

> (**WINNIFRED** *withdraws, and is gone.*)

> (**SIR ARTHUR** *gets up.*)

SIR ARTHUR. Well!
It's a beautiful day outside, lots of things to be done.
Run along boys,
sun'll go out one of these days
(scientists say)
so
get some sun.

FRANK. *(This is it!)* Wait – just before –
you started to say –
What was it you were thinking about, sir?

SIR ARTHUR. Ah!!
Good boy, good reminder,
was just thinking
let's take the horses out later
give this old man some exercise.

FRANK. The horses...

SIR ARTHUR. Yeah, horses and dogs...

FRANK. There wasn't anything else you were going to...?

SIR ARTHUR. No, don't think so...

> *(He senses but doesn't understand* FRANK's *disappointment.)*

No horses today?

FRANK. No, yeah, of course yes. Love it.

SIR ARTHUR. Great! See you later.

> *(He lumbers off, digestif in hand, and is gone. A beat.* FRANK *is deflated.* CUDDY *can't help himself:)*

CUDDY. How are you feeling?

FRANK. What's it to you?

CUDDY. Your head is OK? Nothing hurts?

FRANK. No...why?

CUDDY. Oh...there's just been something going around. That's all.

> *(A weird beat.)*

FRANK. How's the...Morris dancing?

CUDDY. Great.

FRANK. ...Great.

> (**FRANK** *is going to leave – and* **CUDDY** *can't help himself, it just bursts out:*)

CUDDY. You don't really agree with the old man.

FRANK. I like the way your father thinks.

CUDDY. Or do you like the way you *think* he's thinking about you?

FRANK. I'm not sure what you mean.

CUDDY. Well,
I think you *think* he's looking for a son.
But I think you *forgot* that he already *has* one.
Don't you know you're wasting your time?

FRANK. I think you might be asking the wrong question actually.

CUDDY. *(A little breathless.)* Oh yeah?

> (**FRANK** *steps close to* **CUDDY***. So close. So close that they could kiss. The electricity sparks up.* **CUDDY** *is a little light-headed with it, and* **FRANK** *knows.*)

FRANK. Like maybe
you should be asking *why* it is
that even though your dad has a son
(technically, you are technically the son)
he needs to find a better one.

CUDDY. *(Rage and longing.)* *I'm* the heir, Frank.

FRANK. ...Are you sure?

> (*He is so close to* **CUDDY**'s *mouth that* **CUDDY** *is a little dazed.*)

Sometimes we can get complacent
we can get complacent about what we have
and we just assume we can get what we want
but actually we *can't* anymore, actually
even if we were born in a *castle*
even if we have *hobbies*
like *Morris* dancing, for example
even in those cases sometimes,
deals are made, rules get changed, and
we start to lose things.

> (**CUDDY** *moves to close the distance between them, to kiss* **FRANK**. **FRANK** *side-steps him neatly.*)

Hope things work out for you, Cuddy.

> (**FRANK** *saunters out of the banquet hall, like a million bucks.* **CUDDY** *stares after him, bruised and seething.*)

CUDDY. I'm gonna kill him.

6.

(**ELIZABETH**'s *cottage. Later. Day.*)

(**SCRATCH** *is back. A little jittery, just arrived.*)

SCRATCH. I thought it would help if you could sort of – see what you're getting. All the services provided.

ELIZABETH. I said No.

SCRATCH. Yes but you see
the thing is
nobody says No.

ELIZABETH. I did.

SCRATCH. But that's because you don't understand the value of the offer. I don't want to boast, but I've only been doing this a few hundred years and yet I recently got a promotion, and honestly? The secret to my success is authenticity. My offer is authentic. It is detailed and it is authentic and people are statistically, authentically happy when they work with me.

ELIZABETH. How experienced are you?

SCRATCH. I'm *fast-rising.* If you want to get detailed, my year-end numbers are better (across the board) than my senior colleagues', and my customer satisfaction is generally a good seven to ten points higher. If you heard me out, you might be surprised.

(*A moment. Has he scored a point? Just in case he has, he rushes forward:*)

So, here is a list of all the townfolk who have been cruel to you or said cruel things or acted impolitely. Their names, their addresses, the degree of their offense. I arranged it in a few different ways, there's sort of youngest-to-oldest (that's this one), and then there is meanest-to-least-mean (that's this one), and then

I arranged it in order of the kinds of punishments I might suggest, and that list is structured in order of my favorite-to-least-favorite punishments.

(A moment.)

Would you like to hear some of my favorite punishments?

(ELIZABETH *is intrigued despite herself.)*

ELIZABETH. *(But this is a Yes.)* Can I stop you?

SCRATCH. *(Brightly.)* Okay! Great! Here we go!
Pox on the cow.
Pox on the hens.
Pox on the baby.
That's the pox section.

(Pause.)

Milkmaid is ornery.
Girlfriend is ornery.
Wife is ornery.
That's the Personal Relationship section.

(Pause.)

Ants.
Crickets.
Lice.
That's the insect section.
Are you still with me?

ELIZABETH. Those are all a bit...juvenile.

SCRATCH. I'm sorry?

ELIZABETH. You don't think?
A bit...under-effective.

SCRATCH. I assure you, they're *very* effective! Imagine: you sneeze and an ant falls out, the internal made external, a metaphor that / I particularly –

ELIZABETH. What about wholesale slaughter?

SCRATCH. Oh.
Well.
That's a thing that we – I mean, that's sort of an advanced offer.
But we *do* do that.
But it tends to be...advanced.

ELIZABETH. Advanced how?
Advanced like that's the deal you make with men?

> *(An awkward moment – that* is *the deal he makes with men.)*

And women get crickets. Okay.

SCRATCH. It sort of just works out like that.

> *(Getting flustered, as she stares at him.)*

It's not –   [about bias]
women have their own –   [set of interests]
and *they* tend to be the ones who ask *me*   [about insects]
so *I'm* not even
but
so
it just generally works out like that.
Unconsciously.

ELIZABETH. Well
maybe if you *consciously* offered women wholesale slaughter more often
it would work out a different way. Generally.

SCRATCH. I guess maybe it might.

> *(A beat. He is intrigued by her.)*

> *(She is intrigued by him and doesn't want to be.)*

ELIZABETH. Is that everything?

SCRATCH. Is that – what do you mean is that everything?

ELIZABETH. Well, are you done? With your pitch?

SCRATCH. Well I guess not, because you didn't like it.

ELIZABETH. I didn't say I didn't like it, I just said it was trivial and I asked about a less trivial version.

SCRATCH. Would you like to hear my less trivial version?

ELIZABETH. Would you like to deliver your less trivial version?

SCRATCH. I wouldn't mind the opportunity.

ELIZABETH. Okay, you're on.

> *(Are they flirting? Both of them are enjoying the interaction and also wary of it.* **SCRATCH** *delivers his next pitch with the energy of flirtation.)*

SCRATCH. Okay.

Okay.

Okay: picture this. A sea of blood. A tsunami rises up. It too, is made of blood. The tsunami of blood crashes down on your village. Those who have scorned you? Taken your place in line at the well? Imagine their faces. Right before the blood wave devours them. They are crying out for help...and then they are gone. You were a victim. You were helpless in the face of their cruelty. Now...you are revenged.

> *(A moment.)*

Yes No?

ELIZABETH. Hm.

SCRATCH. Visual. Poetic.

ELIZABETH. Pitch it to me the way you'd pitch it to a man.

SCRATCH. That *was* –

ELIZABETH. "Visual poetic"? Nope.

You'd appeal to a different sense of self – wouldn't you? – than "visual poetic."

(Seeing that she's scored a point.) I'm standing here – I'm Sir Arthur. I run this town. I have the biggest balls you've ever seen. Pitch it to me now.

> *(Game Time.* **SCRATCH** *gets a whole new kind of serious.)*

SCRATCH. Okay.
Sir Arthur.
It's nice to meet you. I've heard a lot about you.

ELIZABETH. *("As Sir Arthur," but also, with steel.)* Get to the point.

SCRATCH. The point – Sir Arthur – is I have something that you've always wanted.
And that is: the power to destroy.
It's possible that you think of yourself as a man who builds.
But there is nothing so fully entwined with creation, than the act of destruction.
If I might reference some who have gone before you:
Genghis Khan. A maker of culture, a destroyer of armies.
Alexander the Great. A maker of nations, and a destroyer thereof.
Odysseus. A maker of journeys, and of war.
You, Sir Arthur, were made for greater things than you have yet achieved.
Man cannot be given greatness. He has it or he doesn't.
But he can be given power, with which to exercise his greatness.
And power, sir, is the thing that I bring to the table.

> *(Pause.)*

Are you ready to say yes to history?

(A beat. This has gotten electric and charged.)

(Even though **SCRATCH** *is giving his serious "man version" pitch.)*

(It moves **ELIZABETH** *in a fundamental way, to be addressed like this.)*

ELIZABETH. Yes, that is different.

SCRATCH. Forgive me.
Even the greatest salesman sometimes miscalculates his audience.

ELIZABETH. Is that what happened, do you think? Did you "miscalculate" me?

(Real sparks between them as:)

SCRATCH. I think everybody miscalculates you.
And I think they do it all the time.
But I won't make that mistake again.

*(***ELIZABETH*** feels seen. She has not felt like this at any point that she can remember, and it off-balances her a little.)*

ELIZABETH. Why me?

SCRATCH. You're the talk of the town.

ELIZABETH. You're here because the villagers gossip about me?

SCRATCH. No, I'm here because they gossip about you, and under the gossip they fear you.

ELIZABETH. I've never done anything to them. I barely do anything at all.

SCRATCH. You exist, and that's enough. And people like that – whose sheer existence speaks louder than anything they do or don't do – those people interest me. Broadly speaking.

(Pause, honest:)

SCRATCH. And then you said No.

ELIZABETH. Right.

SCRATCH. And I got even more interested.

(Beat.)

ELIZABETH. *(A certain guarded honesty.)* It's not that I don't want it. What you're selling.

SCRATCH. Yes?

*(A beat, in which **ELIZABETH** almost says any number of things. And then:)*

ELIZABETH. I'll think about it.

7.

(In the castle. **WINNIFRED** *and* **FRANK** *have stolen a moment alone.* **WINNIFRED** *tries to keep her voice down, but sometimes it sparks in indignation. There is a rushed, hushed quality to the scene.)*

WINNIFRED. But when are you getting me a ring?
And when can I start telling people?
And actually, when are you gonna tell Sir Arthur?

FRANK. Whoa whoa whoa
calm down.

WINNIFRED. If Sir Arthur knew we were married, he might be happy.

FRANK. *("You're being so naïve.")* Baby...

WINNIFRED. He never really talks to me but
if he talked to me, he might like me.

FRANK. *("I can't* believe *how naïve you're being.")* Baby.

WINNIFRED. What!

FRANK. I love you. And you love me. And little things like a *ring*, little things like a *dress*, those little things can wait right now. We're playing the smart game. We're playing the long game. And this is the part where we stay quiet. Right?

WINNIFRED. ...I guess.

FRANK. You guess, or I'm right?

(Beat.)

WINNIFRED. I just feel like
sometimes
I forget what the plan is
and then it feels like

we're just drifting farther and farther away from each
other
even though we grew up together and
you married me and
then Sir Arthur invited you here and then
I *came* here for *you*, I became a servant in the castle to
be close to *you*
but
now
I'm like, dusting a portrait
and like, serving drinks,
and you're like, sitting there next to him
at the head of the table
laughing at all his jokes
and pretending you don't know me at *all*,
pretending I'm just the girl who's serving you,
and not the girl who you said you wanted to spend your
whole *life* with
and
then that starts to feel really really sad.

    (A beat.)

FRANK. You know what the plan is.

WINNIFRED. Do I?

FRANK. Come on, of course you do.
When Sir Arthur makes me his heir, I'll be able to do
whatever I want.
You'll be right there with me, we'll run the castle
together – eventually.
But right now, I can't rock the boat.
And, you know, part of that is being, uh, friendly to his
friends' daughters.

WINNIFRED. ...But what if he doesn't make you his heir?

FRANK. *("You're being naïve again.")* Baby.

WINNIFRED. I mean he *has* a son.

FRANK. Cuddy likes *Morris* dancing.

WINNIFRED. Okayyyy but someday he's gonna meet a girl, and –

FRANK. Uhh, yeah, no.

WINNIFRED. How do you know?

FRANK. Believe me.

> *(A beat, faux-casual:)*

WINNIFRED. About those daughters you mentioned...

FRANK. *Okay*, Winn, look –

WINNIFRED. Those *very* important daughters of a station higher / than –

FRANK. C'mon, stop that Winn. It's just part of the plan.

WINNIFRED. Maybe that's the part where the plan starts to suck.

(Low and desperate.) We don't need Sir Arthur, we could go back home –

FRANK. And do what?

> *(His vehemence has silenced her – he tries to find a gentler tone with her:)*

Sweetheart, we have to ask for more than what we were born with.

WINNIFRED. Why?

FRANK. Because if we don't ask for more, we'll end up with less.

WINNIFRED. But right now, I don't even have you.

FRANK. You *have* me, we're just –
ugh, Winn
it's gonna be fine.

(With great care:)

WINNIFRED. Well
I hope so, Frank, because
here's the complicated thing:
I'm pregnant.

FRANK. …You're what??

WINNIFRED. Sorry – I should say:
We
are pregnant.

FRANK. Since when?

WINNIFRED. I wasn't sure for about a week.
And then I became sure.

FRANK. Oh.
Oh my god.

WINNIFRED. That doesn't sound like a good "oh my god."

FRANK. Oh my god.

WINNIFRED. Right.
OK.
Well
let me put it this way.
If your Sir Arthur hooked you up with somebody's rich
daughter,
and you let him,
and then everybody found out you actually have a *wife*
and she's having your *kid*,
I think you might not be as shiny as you are right now,
you know?
You might…tarnish. A little. In the eyes of Sir Arthur.
So. Let's lock it down, Frank Thorney.

*(Something shines in **FRANK** – that cold edge.)*

(He leans in. His aria.)

FRANK. *(Soft, menacing.)* Here's the thing, my love
　　maybe I didn't explain this clearly
　　so let me try it again:

　　Sometimes men come along
　　born under a special star
　　and that's me.
　　I've always known it's going to be different for me.

　　I didn't scrape by for nothing,
　　working the land – that shitty rocky soil,
　　half the time you can't even get a potato out of it,
　　and some winters we get by, but some winters there's
　　just nothing,
　　so we pull our belts tight and wait for spring and then
　　spring comes
　　but actually there's *still* nothing –

　　I don't plan to be nothing.

　　I got by because I could feel what I *could* be
　　just under the ribs, waiting to grow,
　　waiting for the right soil
　　and here it is
　　and here I am
　　and I am ready to be great.

　　You too, if you want greatness,
　　but maybe not you, maybe you don't
　　and that's OK –
　　people grow apart – and that's sad, when it happens,
　　but it does happen.

　　You're gonna be a great wife, Winn
　　and I love you to death but
　　nobody is getting in my way
　　not even you.

WINNIFRED. ...Frank?

(Like a switch being hit, **FRANK** *is himself
again, as she knows him.)*

FRANK. But I'd rather we did it together.

8.

(Elizabeth's cottage. Night.)

*(**ELIZABETH** might be wearing a nightgown.)*

*(She was on her way to bed. **SCRATCH** has surprised her.)*

ELIZABETH. Really?

SCRATCH. You said to come back.

ELIZABETH. It's late.

SCRATCH. Time! is so...

(He gestures: "fluid, confusing," etc.)

ELIZABETH. Also...knocking?

SCRATCH. Knocking...

ELIZABETH. It's polite. You should start doing it.

SCRATCH. Oh!
Knocking.
I'm sorry. I've never... I haven't gotten used to knocking.

ELIZABETH. I've noticed.

SCRATCH. I don't really – *return* to a place. You know? I make the grand entrance – which does not require knocking, which sort of requires the opposite of knocking – and then we conduct good business, and then I'm gone. You're the only person I've ever *re*-visited.

ELIZABETH. That can't be true.

SCRATCH. I swear it.
But! knocking.
Next time, I will knock.

ELIZABETH. *(But, dry, joking.)* I might not invite you back.

SCRATCH. If there were to be a next time, I would knock.

> *(A beat.)*

ELIZABETH. I haven't seen you for a day or two.

SCRATCH. I've been busy.

ELIZABETH. Doing what?

SCRATCH. Hither and thither, making observations, taking notes...did you miss me?

ELIZABETH. Not at all.

SCRATCH. Too bad.

> *(**ELIZABETH** has to crack a smile.)*

ELIZABETH. I suppose you want a drink.

SCRATCH. I wouldn't think of imposing...unless you were going to have one yourself.

ELIZABETH. Well I'm awake now, I might as well.
Have a seat.

> *(As **SCRATCH** sits by the fireplace, and **ELIZABETH** pours them each a drink:)*

So you've been all around the world, seen all the things, kingdoms have fallen and only you remember that they were ever there – would you say that's a fair assessment?

SCRATCH. I'm somewhat well-traveled.

ELIZABETH. Don't tell me you're modest.

SCRATCH. I'm *fairly* well-traveled. Although my senior colleagues get out more, as you'd imagine.

ELIZABETH. *(Joining him.)* And you all wander around the world, you stop in some town, you find some sad slob – then what?

SCRATCH. What do you mean "then what"? You've seen "then what."

ELIZABETH. So you and me – the way you're handling it with me – that's party line?
Nothing special, right? Just "how it's done"?

    (A spark between them.)

SCRATCH. I didn't say that.

    (A beat.)

You know, this might sound a little overblown to you but
the training manual advises us to think of ourselves as sort of
"merchants of hope," if you will
and I think there's actually something to that.
Let's face it, capitalism has its difficulties,
any system of transaction does, but
there's something really satisfying in sitting down with someone
and saying: Tell me what you *hope* for,
and then – (with the right transaction in place) –
making it come true.
But we take different approaches in different circumstances
and you're certainly a
different, uh,
circumstance.

    (A beat between them. This landed. More spark.)

ELIZABETH. Who's your favorite been?

SCRATCH. My favorite what?

ELIZABETH. Person. Transaction. Do you differentiate?

SCRATCH. *(A moment, then.)* I don't... I don't have favorites.

ELIZABETH. But you must have liked somebody more than
    you liked somebody else.

SCRATCH. ...No.

ELIZABETH. Never?

SCRATCH. *(Increasingly thrown.)* I... Well, in the *moment*,
    I suppose...there can be a certain
    occasional connection or
    recognition of some kind or
    interest or...
    but we're certainly not supposed to...
    Not professionally speaking.

> *(Pause, honest:)*

I'm not used to...personal questions.

ELIZABETH. I probably shouldn't pry.

SCRATCH. It's all right.

ELIZABETH. I'm not used to visitors.
    Or conversations.
    So...

SCRATCH. Well, you're doing pretty well so far.

> *(They drink.)*

ELIZABETH. You look very young.

SCRATCH. I know.

ELIZABETH. Did you choose that guise for some practical
    purpose? Or do you just like to look young?

SCRATCH. Do you want the real answer, or the politic
    answer?

ELIZABETH. Do you think you're in the hut of a politic
    person?

> *(**SCRATCH** acknowledges the humor.)*

SCRATCH. *(A little self-conscious.)* Well, there is something about young men. A certain...luminosity, if you know what I mean. A young man is a creature with a whole future ahead of him, and things might be hard for him at some point, but generally he will succeed, and the hard things will only be the things he had to master on his way to success. So when you look at a young man, who is making you an offer – you feel good inside, subconsciously I mean, you feel like you are participating in a story about possibility and a bright future. You feel like maybe those things could apply to you too. Do you know what I mean?

ELIZABETH. *(Soft.)* Yes I know what you mean.

SCRATCH. Does it tarnish the picture for you, hearing the reasoning behind it?

> (**ELIZABETH** *looks at him closely.)*

ELIZABETH. No, I still feel it. A certain...aura of success. It's palpable.

SCRATCH. You know, I used to appear as a woman much more often, back in the day. First I tried being very beautiful, and then I tried being much older, kind of weathered. And then I just stopped altogether and I started being a man.

ELIZABETH. Why did you stop?

SCRATCH. *(Honest.)* I didn't like how people looked at me. Day to day, being looked at with a kind of...
I don't know, either way it got under my skin, I had to stop.

> *(A moment, in which her silence speaks. He realizes:)*

I'm so sorry.
That was –
indelicate / I'm sorry.

ELIZABETH. *(A little raw.)* Why are you sorry? That's your
whole pitch, isn't it?
All the ways that people look at me, all those sad ugly
ways – I could upgrade for the price of a soul?

SCRATCH. Yes...but I wasn't making a pitch right then. We
were just...having a nightcap.

ELIZABETH. *(Genuinely probing.)* Are we? "Just"?

SCRATCH. There's a time and a place for business. I
thought we were off the clock right now.
Tell me if I'm wrong?

(This means something to her.)

ELIZABETH. ...No.
Let's keep it...off the clock.

(The air changes.)

SCRATCH. Cheers to off the clock.

ELIZABETH. Cheers.

(Pause.)

SCRATCH. Why haven't you ever left?

ELIZABETH. Where would I go?

SCRATCH. There are so many places, I don't know how to
answer that.

ELIZABETH. But you need a ticket, yes? to go anywhere.
Or a horse, or a donkey, or a donkey-cart.
And for any of those things, you need money.
And for money you need an income, and for an income
you need employment
and for employment, you need employers
and for employers, the first thing you need
is not *skill*, contrary to what you would think
(skill is acquired after all)
but a *reputation*.

SCRATCH. You've thought about this.

ELIZABETH. No, I've lived it.

> *(Beat.)*

I used to be a maid in the castle, when Sir Arthur's father was alive.

SCRATCH. I didn't know.

ELIZABETH. It was a long time ago. And it didn't end well.

> *(Beat.)*

Sir Arthur and I were... There was a time...
Very young, very stupid, but...
I thought we'd get married and then it wouldn't matter, the whole thing of my reputation.

> *(Beat.)*

We didn't, as you can see, get married.

SCRATCH. Ah.

ELIZABETH. Or rather, *he* did. Just not to me.

> *(Beat.)*

It made me very unwelcome at the castle, and later in the village, understandably.
Deflowered, etc. Tarnished.
How easily we jump from tarnished to untouchable.

SCRATCH. *(Means it.)* I'm sorry.

ELIZABETH. It's so strange to talk about myself.

SCRATCH. Am I prying?

ELIZABETH. Yes, but don't you mean to be?

SCRATCH. A little, but I'll stop if you're uncomfortable.

ELIZABETH. I'm not uncomfortable.

(A pause, and then **ELIZABETH** *sort of blurts:)*

ELIZABETH. You're very good-looking.

SCRATCH. *(Startled, a little flushed.)* I change shapes, as
we / discussed –

ELIZABETH. Discussed, yes, we did.

SCRATCH. So it's cheating. You know?
I'm not luck-of-the-draw. I just chose this one.

ELIZABETH. Some people know how to dress themselves.
That's a skill-set too.
Wouldn't you say?

SCRATCH. I don't like compliments.

ELIZABETH. Just say: Thank you.

SCRATCH. *(After a moment.)* Thank you.

9.

(The banquet hall, with its dead-wife portrait.)

(The end of a banquet.)

(SIR ARTHUR. CUDDY. FRANK. *The tension in the room is palpable.* **WINNIFRED** *clearing dishes, slamming them around.)*

SIR ARTHUR. For example, Sir John's youngest
she took quite a liking to you, Frank.
She took a liking.

FRANK. She was very friendly.

SIR ARTHUR. She's a good woman
that whole pack of them
good women.
It does an old man good to see two young people
talking together like that.

> **(WINNIFRED** *shoots* **FRANK** *a look – he ignores her.)*

FRANK. Thanks so much for introducing us.

SIR ARTHUR. You know my old man used to say:
"A meeting like that, can only end in a marriage."
I used to be like: Dad! You're embarrassing me!
But now I know – old men, we got x-ray eyes.
Now, if Cuddy would let me introduce him to some of
her sisters –

CUDDY. *(Blurts out, in the moment.)* I'm seeing someone.

SIR ARTHUR. *(Hopeful, thrilled.)* Are you now!

FRANK. Oh I didn't know that.

CUDDY. *(Oh shit.)* ...Yeah, I've been seeing someone. So.

SIR ARTHUR. Good lad, good lad.
Well who is she?

CUDDY. Well...we're keeping it on the DL at the moment.

FRANK. Uh-huh.

SIR ARTHUR. You should bring her home
bring her to dinner
let your old dad meet her.

CUDDY. Yeah, definitely
later, definitely later.

SIR ARTHUR. Tell her your old dad isn't so scary, not so bad
ask Frank here, I raised him like a son
man in the castle isn't so scary, is he now?
Winnifred!
Do you have those mints, those mints that I –? [like]

(**WINNIFRED** *comes over with mints.*)

There we go, thank you Winnifred.

FRANK. So where'd you meet?

CUDDY. Sorry?

FRANK. Just wondering where you met this, uh, girl, that's all.

CUDDY. What's it to you?

FRANK. I mean, I'm just wondering if she's a
Morris dancer
or
I don't know, are we talking a servant, or
maybe in the stables –

SIR ARTHUR. *(Laughing, how silly!)* Girls don't work in
the stables, Frank.

FRANK. *(Staring straight at* **CUDDY.***)* Oh yeah. I guess
they don't.
I guess girls *don't* work in the stables.
Silly me.

CUDDY. How's *your* love-life, Frank? Sounds like you met someone too.

FRANK. Well I was lucky to meet Sir Arthur's friends, have some great conversations...

SIR ARTHUR. *(To* **FRANK.***)* Don't be modest, Frank, the girl couldn't take her eyes off you...or her hands!

> *(Crash!* **WINNIFRED** *slams a platter.)*

FRANK. *(Avoiding* **WINNIFRED***'s eyes.)* She's just enthusiastic.

SIR ARTHUR. We should have her and Sir John over
and Cuddy, you can invite your girl, sooner the better!
Have all the ladies to dinner
whaddaya say, boys?

> *(**FRANK** and **CUDDY** are both reluctant, for their own reasons.)*

FRANK. Well...

CUDDY. Yeah sometime maybe.

FRANK. Maybe later.

SIR ARTHUR. If you're gonna be that shy, somebody else will swoop in
trust me, you can't be shy in this business
gotta set your sights and then –
ZING!
like an arrow.
Cuddy's mom –
she was the prettiest girl in the room
and I coulda hung back
I coulda been shy
I coulda been like, "Why would a girl like that talk to a guy like me?"
but no
I set my sights and
ZING!

went right over.
A month later, we were married.

FRANK. Sure...sure...

CUDDY. Of course...

SIR ARTHUR. *(Nostalgia takes him over.)* On our wedding
day I said, "You sure about this?"
Cuz it all went kind of fast, you know, I got cold feet,
I said, "Are you gonna love me when we're old?" And
she looked me straight in the eye and said:
"Are you gonna give me a reason to love you?"

(Laughing, genuine relish.) That woman! She never let
you off the hook
and you never wanted to be
off the hook
you never even wanted to be.

> *(A moment that is strange because in it,* **SIR**
> **ARTHUR** *feels the depths of his loss all over*
> *again. And* **FRANK** *and* **CUDDY** *eye each*
> *other, each dissatisfied with how this all went,*
> *each not sure what to do next. The moment is*
> *broken when* **SIR ARTHUR** *stirs himself.)*

Well! That's enough of that.
Winnifred! My glasses, if you would?

> *(***WINNIFRED** *produces them.)*

Paper?

> *(She produces it.)*

Bless you, Winnifred.
Boys.

> *(***SIR ARTHUR** *and* **WINNIFRED** *exit.)*

> *(A laden beat between* **FRANK** *and* **CUDDY**.*)*

(FRANK sits facing away from CUDDY, refusing to acknowledge him. He finishes his drink. That hot feeling surges up in CUDDY, anger and resentment and everything else, it surges so high he can't hold his tongue.)

CUDDY. My dad's gonna get tired of you.

FRANK. *(Not turning.)* I don't think so.

CUDDY. When he plucked you out of a field, philanthropy was in vogue.
Watch out, it's going out of style again.

FRANK. You gotta set your sights and then ZING, Cuddy you heard the old man say so.
Not my fault that you don't have any ZING in you.

CUDDY. You'd be surprised how much Zing I have.

FRANK. Here's the thing, Cuddy.
Every time your dad looks at me he sees the best version of himself. And every time he looks at you, he sees all his failures staring back at him.
Which of us do you think he wants to look at?

(The hot feeling surges into murder. CUDDY flings himself at FRANK, maybe trying to put hands around his neck. Whatever the gesture is, FRANK subdues him quickly, pushing him back with a laugh. CUDDY surges forward again, and FRANK puts a hand square on CUDDY's chest and pushes him backward. A moment. CUDDY's rage doesn't melt, but it is confused by a bolt of pure longing. Without knowing what he's going to do, he puts his hand on FRANK's chest. Is it a shove? Will it become one? Neither of them really knows. A moment that is confused and raw and full of possibility and also weird and awkward. And then WINNIFRED re-enters.)

WINNIFRED. BOYS.

> *(They jolt apart.)*

I'm cleaning up your banquet
so
maybe you could take this
outside.

FRANK. I was just leaving.

> *(He walks past* **WINNIFRED** *and out.)*

> *(A beat.)*

> *(***CUDDY*** *sinks back into his chair.)*

> *(He puts his head in his hands.)*

WINNIFRED. *(Can't help it.)* ...Are you OK?

> *(All of this comes pouring out of* **CUDDY***:)*

CUDDY. I hate him.

WINNIFRED. ...I know.

CUDDY. Sometimes I really fucking hate him
the way he takes up space and
sort of sprawls around and
the way he *talks*
and –

WINNIFRED. I know.

CUDDY. And then also I wanna just
put my hands around his throat and
squeeze and then
I want to mash my face into his face
and I want to be *so close* to him
I want to *wear* him.

WINNIFRED. I know what that's like.

(**CUDDY** *looks up at her.*)

CUDDY. Yeah I bet you do.

(*A beat between them.*)

WINNIFRED. So you know about us?

CUDDY. Yeah.

WINNIFRED. (*With hope.*) Did Frank tell you?

CUDDY. No.

WINNIFRED. Oh.

How do you know?

(**CUDDY** *hesitates. Still hopeful:*)

Is it like...is there sort of an energy between us?
Like you can just tell by looking at us that there's an
unbreakable connection?

CUDDY. ...No.

WINNIFRED. Oh.

CUDDY. The devil told me, actually?

WINNIFRED. ...The devil?

CUDDY. Yeah.

WINNIFRED. Oh.

CUDDY. We were just talking. And we ended up talking
about Frank. And he told me about you guys. This is all
cone-of-silence.

WINNIFRED. Okay...

CUDDY. Actually the whole thing is, the whole mashing-
my-face-into –
my whole Frank thing is also cone-of-silence.

WINNIFRED. Well, me too.

CUDDY. Oh yeah
I guess that's right
you too.

>*(Beat.)*

WINNIFRED. What else did the devil say?

>*(A conflicted beat. **CUDDY** struggles, and then:)*

CUDDY. I asked him for something and... He said OK.

WINNIFRED. OK...

CUDDY. And sometimes I'm so glad that I asked for it,
and sometimes I think it's not gonna happen, unless I
make it happen,
but then
sometimes
I guess I wish that I hadn't asked for that thing at all.
And I feel sad. And I feel kinda sick.
Uh –
Do you know what I mean?

WINNIFRED. No.

>*(Pause.)*

What did you ask for?

CUDDY. *(Almost tells her and then.)* It's complicated.

>*(Pause – can't hold back:)*

I just don't understand how you can wanna murder
someone and then also want them to be closer to you
than your own skin.
I mean
is that love? is that hate?
Like, what even *is* that?
Is that how you feel?

WINNIFRED. I think I used to feel like that, but lately I feel
   really sad.

CUDDY. Oh.

WINNIFRED. Really sad and really cold
   like it's constantly five degrees colder than I want it to
   be
   I mean I know it's *not*
   I know it's totally just me
   but that's how I feel.

CUDDY. I'm sorry.

WINNIFRED. It's not your fault.

   (Beat.)

CUDDY. Would you like to marry me?

WINNIFRED. ...I'm sorry?

CUDDY. I mean. I'm not...probably ideal for you, in some
   ways,
   (like, the most obvious ways)
   but in others, I'm really great.
   I have money, I have land, I have a title
   and you don't have to worry about me lying to you
   or sleeping with other women.

WINNIFRED. Um...
   are you kidding or serious?

CUDDY. I'm serious.
   I'm really serious.

WINNIFRED. Oh. I mean.
   That's so nice of you
   but
   your inheritance...?

CUDDY. We'd need to have a kid to lock it in, but after
   that...

WINNIFRED. A kid...

CUDDY. You could sort of do you, and I could sort of do me.

WINNIFRED. Your dad is really not gonna want you to marry the maid.

CUDDY. Honestly, my dad is gonna be *so* happy to see me marry someone and have a kid, that it shouldn't be as much of a problem as you'd think it might be.

(A beat. She didn't intend to say this, but:)

WINNIFRED. Frank used to be so different with me.

CUDDY. Did he?

WINNIFRED. So different, it's like he isn't even the same person now.
We came here, and he just became so different.
But maybe something could happen and he could... change back? Do you think?
I keep thinking that some morning maybe I'll wake up and it'll be like it was, he'll come down to breakfast and just...be himself.
I guess I keep waiting for that.

CUDDY. *(Gentle.)* I think that ship has sailed.

WINNIFRED. How do you know?

CUDDY. Access is a drug, Winnifred.
Once people have it, they don't usually choose to unhook themselves.

(A beat. She knows he's right.)

WINNIFRED. Can I think about this?

CUDDY. OK. But like...
how much time do you need?

WINNIFRED. I'm not sure. I mean. A little bit.

CUDDY. OK...

WINNIFRED. I mean it's a real decision, Cuddy, I need to think about it.

CUDDY. It seems like a pretty good deal to me.

WINNIFRED. Sure, I mean it is, but also
there was a time in which Frank loved me
and he looked at me in this way
that was sort of like an x-ray
except it was an x-ray of him and not of me
so when I saw him looking at me like that
I could read clear desire down to his bones.
And that's a way of being looked at that is...*life*.
It's a bolt of life going all the way through you.
And that's something you're asking me to give up.
And I'm not saying it's a bad trade but
it's a trade.

> *(A moment.)*

CUDDY. Well...think about it.

WINNIFRED. OK.

CUDDY. But think fast.

10.

(Elizabeth's cottage. Night.)

(**ELIZABETH** *and* **SCRATCH**. *The air between them is intimate, easy. Two old friends. Mid-convo.)*

ELIZABETH. – And he said, "A dog"?

SCRATCH. *(Shrugs.)* He wanted to be a dog.

ELIZABETH. That seems like aiming pretty low.

SCRATCH. You know, that's what I thought too. But then it's like: I don't know. Dogs roam in packs. They're happy anywhere. They need very little. They always have friends. When one dog meets another dog, all it takes is a few sniffs and there you go. Humans take years to make friends, and even then...

ELIZABETH. But dogs turn on each other over nothing, over a scrap or a bone.

SCRATCH. So do humans.

ELIZABETH. I've never had any friends, I assumed it would be different with friends.

SCRATCH. Believe me, it rarely is. The statistic I heard was that, of every hundred friends you have, only trust one. But I guess that could be a changing number.

ELIZABETH. Who has a hundred friends??

SCRATCH. Statistically speaking.

ELIZABETH. What if you just have one friend?

SCRATCH. Then, statistically speaking, trust only one-hundredth of that friend.

Or trust him every one hundred days?

Math was never my strong suit.

ELIZABETH. So what are the rules?

SCRATCH. Pretty simple – you're part of a client-list, you get one thing, you have to commit to the thing you got. It used to be more lax, but then you had all these people, they're like, "Well when I said I wanted X, I meant Y," and, "Well when I asked for Y, I didn't think it came with Z," and then you're basically just doing returns all the time, and how can you advance in sales if you're always doing returns? Bad business.

ELIZABETH. Right.

SCRATCH. So then we got more hardcore about it, like across the line, and you'd think sales might drop because people would be more cautious (because, no take-backs), but actually sales soared.

ELIZABETH. Huh.

SCRATCH. And you know what. The guy who became a dog? He was really satisfied.

ELIZABETH. Did you ever see him again?

SCRATCH. Once, by accident. I was making a sale by a junkyard, and this dog comes running around the side of the shed, kinda mangy-looking by now, torn left ear, but with an air of real confidence. And he comes to a stop and looks straight at me. And it was him! And we looked at each other, and then he smiled, and he ran off.

ELIZABETH. I guess it worked out.

SCRATCH. I think a lot of things can work out if people just commit.

ELIZABETH. *(Carefully – she's thought a lot about this.)* I don't think
if I did it
that I would ask to *be* anything else.

SCRATCH. No?

ELIZABETH. I don't think so, no.
And I don't think it would be about *having*.

(**SCRATCH** *is alert now. He can feel that the air has changed, but he stays casual, letting* **ELIZABETH** *lead them wherever they're going to go.*)

SCRATCH. Well...that's two of the main ones.

ELIZABETH. I think
I would want
to *do* something.

SCRATCH. Do you know what you'd do?

(*Beat. An uneasy energy in the room now. Something hot and sharp between them.*)

Look, if you don't want to sell me your soul, that's fine. But I don't really understand why you'd choose a thing you never use, over something you *would* use, something you actually need.

ELIZABETH. Are you trying to make your pitch, or are we off the clock?

SCRATCH. (*A little stung.*) Are you kidding me right now? When in the past week have we been *on* the clock?

ELIZABETH. I don't know, that isn't always something I can tell, precisely.

SCRATCH. Off the clock, we're off the damn clock, we *have been* and continue to be, and if you didn't already know that, then...

ELIZABETH. (*Gentler.*) You can't keep being off the clock, you won't make any sales.

(**SCRATCH** *shrugs.*)

Be honest. You're over at my place and we're up all night talking shit, hanging around all day, how are you getting anything done?

SCRATCH. I'm not.

ELIZABETH. Isn't that a problem?

SCRATCH. I don't know.

ELIZABETH. OK...

SCRATCH. I don't really care.

ELIZABETH. You're a junior salesman, you're supposed to care. How do you think people get to "senior salesman"?

SCRATCH. *(Gesturing between them.)* Look... This doesn't happen that often. Not like this.
So I just...this is just what I want to do. That's all.

ELIZABETH. *(This means a lot to her.)* Oh.

SCRATCH. I hope that's OK.

ELIZABETH. It's OK.

SCRATCH. OK.

(A beat between them. Then:)

ELIZABETH. Do you want an honest answer? To your question?

SCRATCH. Please.

ELIZABETH. There is so much bullshit to put up with.
There are so many times in which I'm right here, I'm right here, and people look through me like I'm empty air. There are so many times in which I say something, and people act like they didn't hear me. Or they *mis*hear me, purposefully, we're down at the well and they say, "The witch is muttering," they say, "The witch cast a spell." I didn't cast a spell, I said, "Can you please move your bucket?" There are so many times in which I want to say something and then I don't – because there's a voice in my head, it says, "What's the use?" And I *want* to want to speak, but I get so tired, I just get so tired that in the end it's easier not to.
And the thing I know I have – the *only* thing – is whatever I have inside me.

The thing that makes people so uncomfortable, the thing they don't want to look too closely at, the thing they don't want to listen to – what if that thing is my soul, and then I give it away? And then they win?
And I don't expect you to understand that, but that's why.
It's not a good reason, but it's the one I have.

> *(A long beat.* **SCRATCH** *is genuinely moved by this. After a moment:)*

SCRATCH. It's good.

ELIZABETH. Sorry?

SCRATCH. It's a good reason.

> *(A moment. He moves closer to her. She lets him. Is he going to kiss her? Does she want him to? She isn't sure. She doesn't move at all. In the end, he sits on the ground. He leans against her. Maybe his head is in her lap. After a moment, she puts her hand on his head.)*

I've never met anyone like you before.

ELIZABETH. That's dumb, you've been all over the world.

SCRATCH. I've never felt this way about anyone.

ELIZABETH. It'll pass. In the whole history of humankind, it always does.

SCRATCH. I'm not human.

11.

(The banquet hall, but this time it's empty.)

*(**SIR ARTHUR** sits alone in his chair.)*

(This is his aria. He addresses the framed portrait of his dead wife.)

SIR ARTHUR. Well
update from the field is:
the boy is getting bigger.

Uh
he's not very much like me
I guess he's more like you
in the eyes
but also he's not really like you either
which sort of *demands* that one
take him for himself alone
which, uh,
is harder for me than it generally was for you.

Frank is doing well!
you would have liked him, he's really...
he's a go-getter
which mattered less to you than it does to me, but
he's also very funny,
he reminds me of you, a little,
I'm not sure why
maybe how it feels to be around him
which is: you generally feel like you're more interesting
than you thought you were –
which is: how I felt around you.

Um

The castle is...
a castle

and

not to be...   [dramatic]
but it still feels
empty
so...

that's a thing. An everyday sort of thing.

(Beat – a burst:)

I don't wear your clothes anymore!
I know I told you that I used to
sneak into your room and put on your clothes
and stand in front of the mirror
and see if I could see you in me
and
I guess I did that for a few years after you died
maybe five years
or six years
or maybe I guess until our boy was
about ten or eleven but
then I stopped.
I think I told you that I stopped before I actually stopped.
But then I did actually stop, so...

What else.

(This also bursts out:)

I don't know how to raise a boy
in this world.
What do I teach him?
If I let him be gentle
he'll just be hurt by someone down the line.
Nobody trusts boys who are gentle,
it brings out everybody's hidden cruelty.
So I tell him, *Be tough, be tough*
and I watch this sort of

blunt thing grow in his eyes
like he's disappointed in how disappointed I am
but
if he could just *be tough* then I would know
that I'm raising him well enough to get by
and then I could worry about: Is he Gentle enough
and that could be like a
luxury worry
like, "Does he know how to be Kind"
like, that could be something
from time to time I would remind him
to be Kind
all the while knowing that
he will survive, he will survive, he will outlast me.

And also we can't talk to each other.
Frank and I can talk to each other!
We talk all the time!
We talk about falcons and hunting and
women and
politics and
I don't know
I don't know.

    (This is hard to say out loud, but:)

I don't think
Cuddy
is ever going to give us an heir.
And
I think when we were younger, I had this sort of
Optimism
about him
and about us
and about our future as a family but
I think it was *your* optimism that I had, actually
and now

that's gone
so...

(Surprises himself with this:)

Sometimes I feel like I'm dying
and I know I'm not
but I feel like I am.

(Long beat in which there is so much more he would like to say, but it all seems suddenly futile.)

OK I guess that's all.

12.

(The castle. Banquet scene. As usual.)

*(***WINNIFRED*** *and the dishes, etc. But* **SIR ARTHUR** *has the weight of a secret on his chest, and* **CUDDY** *is in a good mood, a little amped. He's coming from Morris practice. He directs a friendly, beaming energy to* **WINNIFRED** *when she passes.)*

CUDDY. – And I'm not saying I've never *led* Morris practice before, but today was really the first time I've gotten to teach. And basically it just comes down to two basic steps, the first being left-hop, right-hop (and so on) – and the second being a *double* step: left-right left-hop – right-left / right-hop –

SIR ARTHUR. *(Cuts in.)* Cuddy my lad.

CUDDY. ...Yeah?

SIR ARTHUR. I have been thinking.

CUDDY. Okay...?

SIR ARTHUR. About this castle. About this land.
About our family name, and the weight of that name and how each of us, in our own way, contributes to this legacy.

CUDDY & FRANK. OK... / ...um...

SIR ARTHUR. And it's not easy for me to say this, and I know this could be
hurtful
if viewed in the wrong light, but
I hope you can understand the *right* light in which to view this
when I say that I have chosen Frank
to be my heir.

CUDDY. Uhhhh...
What?

FRANK. *(Stunned.)* ...What?

SIR ARTHUR. You are still my son, and an important member of this family, Cuddy.
But a man with two sons has more chance of a *legacy* than a man with one
and
in this particular case
Sir John has made an offer
to Frank
of his daughter.

CUDDY & FRANK. *What?*

> *(At the same time, **WINNIFRED** drops a dish.)*

> *(It shatters. They all turn to look at her.)*

WINNIFRED. *(Dazed.)* Sorry.

> *(The **MEN** turn away and ignore her again.)*

CUDDY. Dad, what are you talking about!

SIR ARTHUR. Hear me out –

FRANK. His *daughter*?

> *(**WINNIFRED** is a little dizzy. She sits down. The **MEN** don't even notice this. She holds her stomach.)*

SIR ARTHUR. I was going to mention that to you earlier, Frank
but I needed a moment to get my thoughts in order.
Cuddy, I know this might seem upsetting
but believe me, it's for your good. *Our* good.
Frank and Sir John's daughter will get married
(we looked at the calendar, Frank,
we were thinking next month but

we should do an avail-check)
but
that will just – clear up some space for *you*, Cuddy.
To just...be you.
Maybe you want to be in a monastery?
Maybe you want to become a sort of...wandering scholar?
Maybe –

CUDDY. *(A pathetic plea.)* But I have a girlfriend.

SIR ARTHUR. Cuddy...

WINNIFRED. *(To* **FRANK,** *low.)* What about us?!

FRANK. *(To* **WINNIFRED.***)* I didn't know...

CUDDY. But I have a girlfriend –!

WINNIFRED. You said the plan was *Us*!

SIR ARTHUR. Cuddy, please believe me, I want you to be / happy –

FRANK. I just need to / think...

CUDDY. – You just haven't met her yet!

SIR ARTHUR. – Your mother would have wanted / you to be happy –

WINNIFRED. Was the plan ever *Us*?

SIR ARTHUR. – but this / family needs a next generation –

FRANK. I just need...

SIR ARTHUR. – And I think Frank's desires (and Frank's *opportunities*) –

WINNIFRED. Look at me!

CUDDY. *(Bursts out.)* I'm marrying Winnifred!

SIR ARTHUR. Cuddy...

CUDDY. Tell them, Winn! Tell them what we said.

(A breath. They look at **WINNIFRED**. *She is silent. Betrayed,* **CUDDY** *swings back to his father.)*

SIR ARTHUR. Cuddy, leave the poor girl alone.

CUDDY. *(To* **SIR ARTHUR**.*)* You can't do this to me.

WINNIFRED. *(Soft.)* Frank…

FRANK. *(To* **WINNIFRED**, *anguished, genuinely asking.)* What do I do?

SIR ARTHUR. You'll still *have* the things you have –

WINNIFRED. Tell him about us.

> *(***FRANK*** is frozen, uncertain.)*

CUDDY. *(Heartbroken.)* You're replacing me.

WINNIFRED. Tell him about me.

SIR ARTHUR. You're being emotional about this, boy!

WINNIFRED. *(To* **FRANK**.*)* Tell him.

SIR ARTHUR. It's about the land –

CUDDY. – Let him have the land! –

WINNIFRED. Are you gonna tell him?

> *(…But* **FRANK** *doesn't know.)*

CUDDY. – I care about our *name* –

SIR ARTHUR. – Son…

CUDDY. – It's the only thing we have in common, that doesn't mean something to you?

WINNIFRED. Frank!!

> *(They all look at her again, surprised.)*

> *(***FRANK*** drops his head. He can't look at her.)*

SIR ARTHUR. What's that?

WINNIFRED. Frank married me.

We're married.

> *(A breathless beat.* **SIR ARTHUR** *looks at* **FRANK.***)*

SIR ARTHUR. What's she talking about?

FRANK. I don't know.

> *(Defeat writes itself across* **WINNIFRED.** *But she tries once more, straight to* **SIR ARTHUR:***)*

WINNIFRED. I know we never talk and
I basically just move dishes and
find your mints and your glasses and your paper but
I'm his wife and I'm having his kid.
It's not an easy thing to say but
it is the truth.

> *(***SIR ARTHUR,** *despite himself, is uneasy.)*

SIR ARTHUR. ...Frank?

FRANK. I told you, I don't know.

SIR ARTHUR. Are you sure...?

FRANK. We've never even spoken.

SIR ARTHUR. I'll ask you one more time.

FRANK. You've given me a new life.

(Straight to **WINNIFRED,** *cold.)* Why would I throw it away for a maid?

> *(***WINNIFRED** *gets up and walks out of the room.)*

SIR ARTHUR. I've always thought the girl was strange.

> *(A beat. He's uncomfortable.* **CUDDY** *is completely shut down.)*

SIR ARTHUR. Well boys,
    I know this was hard but
    I think it was a good talk and
    let's all walk it off, and just...
    I'm gonna just...
    OK! All right! We got this.

        (He makes some sporting gestures that don't
        comfort **CUDDY** *and don't connect with* **FRANK,**
        and then he leaves. A long silence.)

        *(***CUDDY*** *sits, devastated.* **FRANK** *hesitates,*
        watching him. There is nothing cruel in
        FRANK *right now. He feels the weight of*
        CUDDY'*s pain, and it doesn't make him*
        particularly happy.)

FRANK. Not that it probably matters but your dad didn't...
    say anything to me.
    So. It's not like I had any kinda...heads-up, or...

CUDDY. It wasn't about the land.
    I don't actually care if you have the land, or the castle,
    or any of this bullshit – (I just wanted to be a Morris
    dancer) – but his *name...*
    You can't understand, but –

FRANK. *(Quiet.)* I do.

        *(A moment. ***CUDDY*** *looks at him.)*

CUDDY. Yeah?

FRANK. Yeah I understand.

CUDDY. Oh.

FRANK. *(Not mean or flip.)* I'm still gonna take it though.
    I can't not take it.
    But I understand.

(A moment between them. It is stripped of contention – oddly intimate. A recognition of sorts, with the games gone.)

CUDDY. And Winnifred?

FRANK. Well.
She's having my kid.

CUDDY. So that was true?

FRANK. Yeah.

CUDDY. What are you gonna do?

FRANK. Well
I'm gonna marry Sir John's daughter
and take your family name
and get somewhere. Finally I'm gonna get somewhere.
And I guess also I'll feel really shitty for a while
when I think about Winnifred
and I'm gonna have to learn to not think about her
and once I learn that, I think I'll feel okay again.
You know?

CUDDY. Do you love her?

FRANK. Yes, but that matters less than it should.
Do *you* love her?

CUDDY. Have you met me?!

(A moment of shared humor – oddly affectionate:)

FRANK. Look...for what it's worth, maybe now you can get what you want.

CUDDY. I don't think so.

FRANK. Your dad will be off your back, for one thing.
Maybe now you can live it up.

CUDDY. I don't think I'm gonna get what I want.

FRANK. Why not? You wanna be a Morris dancer? Be a
Morris dancer!
You wanna...hang out with whoever? Nobody cares.

CUDDY. Not "whoever."

FRANK. Sorry?

CUDDY. *(With intention.)* Not "whoever," Frank.

> *(A moment between them.* **FRANK** *understands
> what* **CUDDY** *meant. He feels the weight of
> longing directed at him. He's not sure what to
> do with this.)*
>
> *(***CUDDY** *reaches out and touches* **FRANK**'s
> *face. Tender, dangerous.* **CUDDY**'s *thumb over*
> **FRANK**'s *lower lip. A beat. And then:)*

FRANK. I can't.

CUDDY. I know.

FRANK. Your dad, and
everything
pretty much everything
super messy.

CUDDY. I know that.

> *(This is the only thing* **FRANK** *can offer in this
> moment – and as such, the tone is oddly gentle:)*

FRANK. I'll let you fight me.

CUDDY. What?

FRANK. I'll let you fight me.

CUDDY. I don't want to fight you.

FRANK. If you want
you could just
we could just
fight.

CUDDY. *(Really asking.)* Why would I want to fight you?

FRANK. It might help.

CUDDY. How?

FRANK. I've found that generally
violence
helps.

CUDDY. Oh.

FRANK. Generally things start to feel better
when it's simple and focused and
sort of urgent
but we don't have to.
It's just if you want.

> *(**CUDDY** knows this is the only thing **FRANK**
> can give him, and in that light:)*

CUDDY. OK.

FRANK. OK?

CUDDY. I'll take it.

> *(They negotiate their way into this fight.)*

> *(Maybe **CUDDY** sort of pushes **FRANK** and
> waits to see how that feels. Maybe **FRANK**
> encourages **CUDDY** to push him. It's a little bit
> like a dance at first, or like two kids playing.
> It's playful, curious, strange. New for them
> both.)*

> *(It escalates. It becomes wild, reckless, savage,
> continuously inventive. Not slapstick, but
> with a sense of play that always tilts over the
> edge back into danger. Sometimes we aren't
> sure if we're witnessing destruction or a
> seduction. Strange things come to hand and
> are used as weapons, but we believe in the
> danger of these things.)*

(Then the real violence leaks in.)

*(**CUDDY** and **FRANK** are increasingly frenzied. **CUDDY** taps into a violence inside himself that is a revelation, a tidal wave, that sweeps him off his feet. **FRANK** falters in the face of this onslaught. It wasn't what he was expecting.)*

*(And then...this happens quickly, so quickly, faster even than the speed of **CUDDY**'s understanding:)*

*(**CUDDY** kills **FRANK**.)*

*(A moment. **CUDDY** realizes what he's done. He is transfixed. He's frozen. Disbelieving at first. This wasn't what he wanted. Was it?)*

*(**CUDDY** kneels by **FRANK**'s body.)*

*(He is numb. He realizes this is real. It is possible that he touches **FRANK**, that he scrubs blood off his hands. A simple, repetitive gesture of shock. Maybe the gesture takes over. **CUDDY** performs a Morris dance.)*

(This is his aria. He does it just for himself, with no sense that there are any eyes on him. It is about anguish and desire and sorrow and loneliness that is constant and searing, and the sick feeling of victory when you've achieved a thing you wish you hadn't actually done, but you were capable of it nonetheless.)

(It is very strange and uncomfortable and oddly beautiful and sometimes funny and sad. It may not even be a "Morris" dance at all. But it should move us, even as we squirm a little.)

(**CUDDY** *finishes. He stands very still, his chest heaving, out of breath, transported, close to tears.*)

13.

(Elizabeth's cottage, night. **SCRATCH** *is there.)*

(So is **WINNIFRED***. She has just arrived.)*

*(***ELIZABETH*** watches* **WINNIFRED** *with a growing intensity.)*

SCRATCH. *(A little nonplussed.)* What can you *get* for it?

WINNIFRED. Yes.

SCRATCH. You want to sell your soul and you want to know what you can *get* for it.

WINNIFRED. Yes, that's right. What'll you give me?

SCRATCH. ...What do you want?

WINNIFRED. What kinds of things do you offer?

ELIZABETH. *(To* **WINNIFRED***.)* You're doing this all wrong.

WINNIFRED. What did you get?

SCRATCH. Oh, she hasn't... / we haven't...

ELIZABETH. *(Same time, also a little flushed.)* We haven't...

WINNIFRED. *(To* **ELIZABETH***, shocked.)* You *haven't*?

SCRATCH. We're just friends.

ELIZABETH. We're just talking.

WINNIFRED. *("That's so weird.")* ...Oh.

    (A beat.)

SCRATCH. How did you know how to find me, anyway?

WINNIFRED. *(Gesturing to* **ELIZABETH***.)* Everyone says she
    has seven teats and a scar like a pentagram
    and she dances with the devil in the pale moonlight –
    and that's you, right? So...

ELIZABETH. Seriously?

SCRATCH. That didn't come from me.

WINNIFRED. So anyway, here I am.

> *(Beat.)*

ELIZABETH. How's the castle?

WINNIFRED. Drafty.

ELIZABETH. How's Sir Arthur?

WINNIFRED. Exhausting.

ELIZABETH. How's the baby?

SCRATCH. What baby?

> *(The **WOMEN** look at him. He catches up.)*

Oh.
Whoa.
Congrats.

WINNIFRED. *(To **ELIZABETH**.)* You can see it on me?

ELIZABETH. Right when you walked in.

WINNIFRED. Nobody else has noticed yet.

ELIZABETH. I'm particularly observant.
Is it Sir Arthur's?

WINNIFRED. No, Frank. But he's dead now, so –

SCRATCH. Whoa no way.

WINNIFRED. ...You really haven't been keeping up to date.

> *(**SCRATCH** kinda shrugs like, wow guess not.)*

ELIZABETH. And here you are, unwed, disgraced.

WINNIFRED. Oh no. No you don't.

ELIZABETH. Excuse me?

WINNIFRED.   You're looking at me, and you're maybe enjoying a little pity, you're like: "Welcome to the land of the outcasts." But guess what – I'm not gonna end up like you. And that's what this guy is for.

> *(Turning back to* **SCRATCH***; this is her aria, simple, powerful, urgent:)*

I don't want a lot.
I *did*, I *did* want a lot. I wanted Frank –
the way he used to look at me, the way he used to laugh,
the surprises that were little windows into a whole new life together
one our parents weren't capable of,
but we *would* be, we'd figure out how, we'd invent it.

But you know what?
Then I grew up.

So now what I want is this:
I want to stay in the castle
and keep dusting the mantles and cleaning the kitchen,
and I want my kid to be a girl, so people can ignore her
and she can stay safe and quiet and out of the way
and maybe sometime, years from now,
there can be a stable boy or a servant
and they don't have to love each other but they'll get married
and then I'll grow old
and then one day I'll die
and they'll have me buried in the castle churchyard
it doesn't have to be prime real estate, but I'd like it if it was near Frank
(or within earshot, anyway)
(or close enough that if wildflowers grow, in the spring, maybe the same bees that go to his flowers would come to my flowers) –

And if a soul is what that costs, I don't think that's so much, really,
because what's a soul ever done for me?

(A beat.)

SCRATCH. Well I think we can make that work.

ELIZABETH. *That's* your pitch?

WINNIFRED. ...What.

ELIZABETH. All you want is more of the same?

If you're gonna sell your soul, sell it for something better.

WINNIFRED. *(Gestures to their surroundings.)* What, like this?

ELIZABETH. So pick something different, pick a new / thing –

WINNIFRED. There are no new things! There's a certain set of things, and whether you're at the castle or in a hut – they'd still be the same things. And what's more, you know that.

ELIZABETH. That's not true.

WINNIFRED. No?

Let's say I ask the devil to make me – nobility! The top of the heap. The men go out hunting, the men go to war – and there I am, sitting alone at the end of a very long table. And the room is very silent, and there's still nobody listening.

Where's our new world, Elizabeth?

*(A moment. **ELIZABETH** hears this.)*

ELIZABETH. So we have to imagine one, we have to imagine things differently.

WINNIFRED. I can't.

Everything I think of, it looks like what I know.

I can't see what a new world would look like.

(Really asking.) Can you?

*(A beat. **ELIZABETH** tries. She really tries.)*

(And...she can't. Her silence says it all.)

WINNIFRED. If we're smart, we'll take what there is, what we know. We'll carve out a corner, make some concessions, and get by.

That's what I plan to do.

And if you have any sense, you'll do the same thing before the devil moves on.

(Back to **SCRATCH**.*)* So do I sign somewhere? Do we need a lawyer?

How did Cuddy do it?

(**SCRATCH** *has a realization.)*

SCRATCH. Oh.

Oh shit.

WINNIFRED. What?

SCRATCH. I never filed the...

Oh shit.

WINNIFRED. What is it?

SCRATCH. I sort of forgot to...

I sort of got a little sidetracked and...

that whole

(Frank too)

never formally

hmm...

Oops.

(*Shrugs – what can I say.)*

Paperwork!

... No point now?

(Moving on.) I'll stop by the castle tomorrow, we can get the details ironed out.

(*He holds out a hand. They shake.)*

WINNIFRED. I'll be waiting.

(She leaves. **ELIZABETH** *makes her decision.)*

ELIZABETH. OK.

SCRATCH. What's that?

ELIZABETH. I'll sell you my soul if you pull the plug.

SCRATCH. ...I don't understand.

ELIZABETH. Destroy it all and see what grows.
That's what I want.
And you can have my soul.

SCRATCH. What – what about you?

ELIZABETH. A hot wind blows through, and I'm gone.
And everything starts over.

SCRATCH. That's –
Wait, no, that isn't –

ELIZABETH. You said tell you what I want? That's what I want.

SCRATCH. But we could go somewhere – you and I –

ELIZABETH. Scratch –

SCRATCH. I'd quit my job –

ELIZABETH. Scratch.

SCRATCH. No! No deal.

ELIZABETH. I want to sell you my soul.

SCRATCH. I don't want it.

ELIZABETH. Yes you do. You've never wanted one more.

SCRATCH. *(This is true, but...)* Not on those terms.

> *(Beat.)*

ELIZABETH. *(Very gently.)* You've seen civilizations the world over.
You've seen how they rise, how they fall.

This one is done. You can see that, can't you?
We're caught in the web of a thing our parents built
our grandparents and the grandparents of our grandparents
and so we're building it now too.
We don't know how to do anything other than keep building
even as the strands wrap tighter and tighter around our necks,
we keep building.
So if there's no stopping, no changing, no way to escape
then you have to wipe the slate clean and start again.

(She takes his face.)

Let's start again. OK?

SCRATCH. I love you.

ELIZABETH. I believe you.

SCRATCH. Can't that be enough?

ELIZABETH. For what?

SCRATCH. You and me, fuck the rest of them.

ELIZABETH. I can imagine we'd have some real fun. But then one day, maybe a hundred years from now... One day we'll notice that nothing around us seems to have changed, everyone is just as vicious and frightened and banal as they were before. We'll think: *Shouldn't anything at all have changed?* And then at that moment, whenever it comes, we'll think of this moment, right now. We'll think: *Oh. We had the chance to change all of this. We did have it. We just said No.*

14.

*(**SCRATCH**, alone. In a narrow, focused light.)*

(Similar to the way Elizabeth was in the beginning. His aria.)

SCRATCH. I really appreciate everything you've done for me?
but I think I just
am maybe having a little difficulty
at the moment
in this particular industry
and
I don't want this to be like, I'm *quitting*
but
maybe I just
need to take a time-out...?

(Beat.)

I've been thinking about, you know,
what I want to do instead and
I'm not, let's face it, the most *organized*   [person]
which is why, you know, that *paperwork*...   [wasn't on time]
(so sorry about that)
uh
but maybe I just wanna travel for a while.
Like, see the world, and not have to engage in any kind of
transactionary thing, but like
have some croissants and go whale-watching...
And I know things are all falling apart, the whole thing is
coming apart at the seams
which is rife with opportunity, I mean I understand
what kind of
moment we're in
so maybe I'll just go on vacation for a little bit

and then if I start to feel better, maybe I can come back
then
and we can talk about resuming on a part-time basis?
Or like a freelance thing, or...?

    (Beat, without meaning to:)

I'm having a really hard time sleeping.
I just lie awake all night and
there's a particular color that exists
in the span of time right before the sun comes up
this particular shade of blue that's almost bruise
and I see that color every morning now.
And I try to do all these exercises, like I take deep
breaths
or I do the thing where you relax your muscles in
groups
your feet, then your calves, then your thighs,
like you work upward until your brain is relaxed and
you fall asleep –
but every time I get to my heart area, I start to feel like
I'm having a
sort of slow-motion panic attack
for hours
so I never get to the part where you fall asleep.

    (Beat.)

I know you can't really answer this, because
we just should do our jobs, and I get it, entropy is the
point anyway,
but
I have no idea if there's anything better coming down
the pike
or if *this is it*, if this is what it is forever –
but then also,
if this *is* what it is
then shouldn't we just learn to live with it?

Be happy in small ways
Be lucky in small ways?
A person could love a person and
that could be enough
couldn't it?

    (Beat – raw, from the heart:)

But
what if there is something *amazing* ahead
and all we have to do
is burn down everything we know
to get to it?

But maybe these aren't the right questions.

There is a single question that I have been asking myself
over and over again
all night, until everything turns that one alarming color
and all day,
I keep asking myself this question, and...

    (Beat – raw, anguished – a question of sorts:)

I find it so hard to have hope right now.
I just find it so hard to have hope.

    (Blackout.)

End of Play

www.ingramcontent.com/pod-product-compliance
Lightning Source LLC
Jackson TN
JSHW010944310125
78140JS00023B/898

* 9 7 8 0 5 7 3 7 0 8 2 3 7 *